Grandy's Quilt

A Gift for All Seasons

Grandy's Quilt

A Gift for All Seasons

Written by
Reneé Wall Rongen

Illustrated by
Mary Maguire

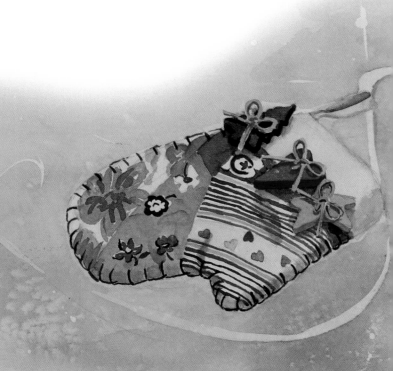

GRANDY'S QUILT: A Gift for All Seasons

ISBN 13: 978-1-931945-12-7

Library of Congress Catalog Number: 2004100526

Printed in The United States of America

First Printing: May 2004

Second Printing: September 2009

13 12 11 10 09   6 5 4 3 2

Expert Publishing, Inc.
14314 Thrush Street NW, Andover, MN 55304-3330
1-877-755-4966
www.expertpublishinginc.com

TO PURCHASE ADDITIONAL COPIES
VISIT OUR WEBSITE AT
www.grandysquilt.com

ACKNOWLEDGEMENTS

Seldom is a book created by one individual and this book is no exception. Talented individuals designed their own square of Grandy's Quilt. Like the blocks of fabric pieced together to make the quilt complete, the book required patches of time and talents to make contributions to the story *Grandy's Quilt: A Gift for All Seasons*.

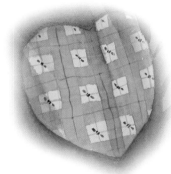

To my husband, Tom: You have always been my biggest cheerleader and my greatest fan. Thank you for your unconditional love and confidence in me.

To my children: Alex, Elizabeth, and Grace, I appreciate your patience posing for silly pictures. Thank you for allowing me to see the quilt through your eyes. Without your words and insight, the quilt would not have enjoyed new life and the book would not have touched so many. I love you all "to the moon and back."

To my Uncle John: Thank you for the encouragement to pursue, preserve, and share the story of Grandy's quilt with others.

To my friend Mrs. Gullekson: Your gift of friendship and your talents as a master quilter gave me inspiration for the book. You are making a difference in the world, one quilt block at a time. I will forever treasure our first meeting at your kitchen table.

Finally, a thank you to *Grandy's Quilt* team:

Therese Bartlett: Your ability to manage the project made it always fun and exciting. You have incredible gifts of patience and humor, both needed to keep the project out front and a joy to be part of. Our rekindled friendship along the way was really the highlight of the book project for me.

Mary Maguire: Your illustrations made *Grandy's Quilt* come alive! You are a very gifted artist and meticulously made sure to get each brush stroke just right.

Ruthmarie Mitsch: Your guidance at the start of this project was invaluable. Thank you for your professionalism and your inspiration.

Harry and Sharron Stockhausen: Thank you for taking me under your wings and prodding me along. Your publishing expertise and encouragement have moved a mountain from under my feet.

In honored memory of my grandmothers,
Lillian Wall and Irene Sullivan,
who shared their quilt blocks of life
with the many who loved them.

"Careful, Tom," I cautioned my husband as he descended the attic ladder yet again, clutching a tattered box. Every year we went through the same ritual. Around the holidays, he brought in the box holding Grandy's quilt. I tried to figure out a way to repair the quilt, in hopes of using it on our bed. Then we put the quilt away for another year. Tom never complained, but I could tell this ritual was getting old.

As I helped him maneuver the box to our bed, I called out to our children. In a flash, Alex, Elizabeth, and Grace ran into the room to join us. They stood wide-eyed as I slowly and delicately removed the lid of the box. With great care, I unfolded the quilt, trying not to pull too hard or snag any loose threads coming from its threadbare top.

"It's sooo beautiful," said Alex, age ten.

"Can I touch it?" eight-year-old Elizabeth asked as she reached for the quilt.

I told them they could touch it if they were careful. "This quilt is very special—and very old," I cautioned them.

Elizabeth and Alex touched the quilt carefully, as if they knew exactly how to show their respect for it. Grace, at age four, chose to show her admiration by playfully pulling the quilt over her head. Watching the children handle the quilt brought me back to the day I received it.

I was the oldest grandchild on my father's side,
and as such, enjoyed a bond with my grandmother,
Grandy, only grandmothers and granddaughters
can share. After Grandy died, my father and
uncle gave me a box of her treasures.

When I held that box close to me, I could tell by
the musty smell that Grandy's old quilt rested inside.

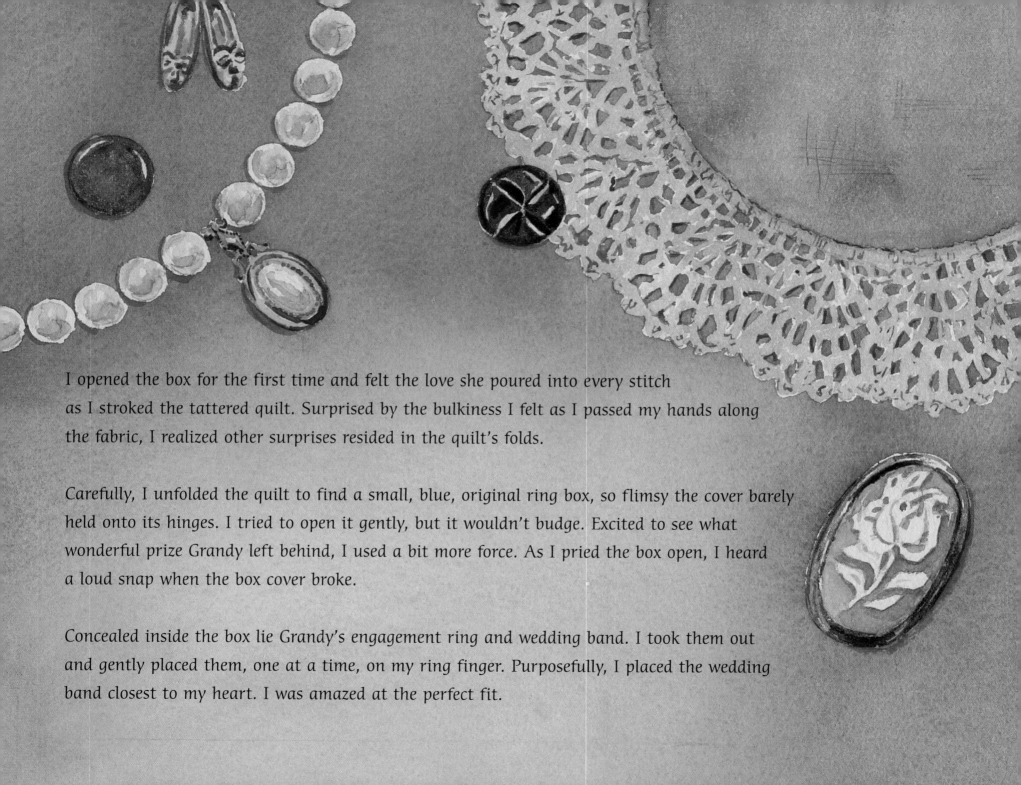

I opened the box for the first time and felt the love she poured into every stitch as I stroked the tattered quilt. Surprised by the bulkiness I felt as I passed my hands along the fabric, I realized other surprises resided in the quilt's folds.

Carefully, I unfolded the quilt to find a small, blue, original ring box, so flimsy the cover barely held onto its hinges. I tried to open it gently, but it wouldn't budge. Excited to see what wonderful prize Grandy left behind, I used a bit more force. As I pried the box open, I heard a loud snap when the box cover broke.

Concealed inside the box lie Grandy's engagement ring and wedding band. I took them out and gently placed them, one at a time, on my ring finger. Purposefully, I placed the wedding band closest to my heart. I was amazed at the perfect fit.

I remembered Grandy had not worn her rings since the aging process stripped her of her precious memories. On occasion, when I visited Grandy, I retrieved her rings from their secret hiding spot in her small room at the nursing home. As I slid each ring over her finger, I softly spoke to her and reminisced, recounting happier chapters of her life.

Now she was gone, and I missed her so much. I glanced down at Grandy's rings on my finger, then turned my attention back to her quilt.

As I touched the little tin wrapped in the quilt next to the ring box, I heard something jingle. The tin was just an old coffee can from the early 1900s. Grandy kept her trinkets of mismatched buttons, old glasses, doilies, charms, and odd pieces of period jewelry in it. I glanced over the collection, then went back to see what else was in the box.

The last treasure hidden inside the quilt was the simple oak cross that hung above Grandy's bed. The cross followed Grandy from the farmhouse to the nursing home and everywhere in between. I clutched the cross and fought back tears, humbled that I was chosen to protect these precious mementos. From the first day I received Grandy's quilt and box of treasures, I knew I would keep the stories surrounding Grandy and her keepsakes alive.

Several winters passed since my father gave me Grandy's treasure box. Each time Tom brought the quilt from the attic, I was transported back to my childhood at the old farmhouse and Grandy's bedroom. Her bedroom was about the size of a shoebox. She kept everything in their calculated places. Since there wasn't enough space in her bedroom for both of us to move around, I stretched out on Grandy's antique wooden bed while we talked. I remember lying there and feeling the soft textures of this same precious quilt beneath me.

Grandy's bed was ebony with inlaid pecan wood tucked inside the dark oak frame. The bed matched the vintage dressing table and bureau. At the impressionable age of ten, I remember how easily Grandy navigated between her dressing table and highboy without missing a step. Of course, I was younger then, but so was Grandy.

She kept many of her belongings behind the three-foot tall door of her corner storage attic. She amazed me at how she could zip in and out of that tiny space without stubbing her toes or bumping into things.

We always talked while I watched her reflection in the dark, oval mirror that allowed a 360 degree span of her bedroom. I never figured out how she stepped so elegantly over the side of her squeaky bed, or squeezed by the German trunk stored at the foot of her bed, without hurting herself. As graceful as a gazelle, she leapt over the hot water heater to reach her final destination without missing a beat of our conversation.

While we talked, I brushed my hair with the emerald-green brush and comb set she received as a wedding gift. After completing my 100 strokes, I picked up the matching oval hand mirror to see if my hair had become magically shinier. In keeping with Grandy's requirement for having everything in its place, I always replaced her wedding gift set on the crisp, white doily that lie across her dressing table.

I watched my children as they anticipated how to gently touch Grandy's fragile quilt that lie on the bed. I didn't know which made me smile more—my children with Grandy's quilt or my childhood memories of Grandy and her quilt. What I did know was that it was time to stop bringing the quilt in every year only to put it back. I was ready to begin my quest of restoring Grandy's quilt.

Thoughts of Grandy's quilt restored and lying across my own bed consumed me. Referred to a number of master quilters, I began the task of calling the women on the list to set up appointments for each of them to view the quilt so I could garner their expertise. I needed to know what the restoration process involved. I also wondered about the cost, but realized that really didn't matter. I just wanted Grandy's quilt restored.

I remember one master quilter's response, "Honey, I can see how much you want to restore this quilt and make it usable again, but I have never come across a quilt that was in such disrepair."

"Couldn't you try something to make it usable again?" I pleaded.

"The backing is completely shot. For me to start taking it apart and piecing it back together is more than I am capable of," she replied.

"Do you know anyone on this list, or maybe have the name of someone else who could?" I pulled out the wrinkled list of master quilters from my coat pocket for her to see.

She ran her fingers down the list and said, "Perhaps Faith Erickson would know what to do. If she can't repair and restore it, no one can. She's the most talented quilter in the region. Better yet, I'll ring her up right now if you would like."

If I'd like? Of course, I'd like, I thought.

I heard her in the other room, "Say, Faith, this is Alma Peterson. I've a young woman here with a quilt she inherited from her grandmother and, unfortunately, it looks in tough shape." As she wrapped the phone cord around her fingers, Alma was almost whispering, "Yes, Faith, I told her I was uncomfortable with it. Could you do her a favor and take a look at it anyway?" Motioning me in, Alma said, "Can you run over there right now, honey? Mrs. Erickson could take a quick look if you can go now."

Encouraged, I nodded yes.

Alma finished up on the phone with Mrs. Erickson, jotted down the directions for me, and wished me luck. I thanked her for sending me in the right direction.

I felt renewed hope as I bounded up the cracked cement steps to Mrs. Erickson's small cottage home and rang her doorbell. The door opened slowly and a pleasant lady looked back at me.

"Hello. Are you Mrs. Erickson?"

"Yes. You find the place okay? That didn't take you long," she said in her Scandinavian accent.

"I hope I'm not inconveniencing you too much."

"No, no. Show me what you have."

I took the quilt out, and she laid it across the worktable in her sewing room.

"Hmm" is all she said as she gently smoothed out what was left of Grandy's quilt. She walked her fingers delicately over the entire quilt as if touching a piece of fine art. Next, she pulled in various spots as if testing it for strength. Then she lifted the quilt up to her nose to smell it. Finally, she gently turned it over.

It seemed like the longest five minutes of my life as I watched her caress the quilt. Finally, she turned to me, "I wish I could tell you something different. It is too frayed and flimsy to do much repair. Perhaps you could find someone to make the salvageable pieces into a wall hanging or table runner."

She handed Grandy's quilt back to me. I hung my head in disappointment and quietly thanked her. I'm sure I didn't seem gracious. I hoped I wasn't rude.

After several conversations with various other master quilters, I temporarily gave up on my idea of restoring Grandy's quilt. However, I still wasn't convinced it couldn't be restored. Placing the quilt back in the original box, I climbed the ladder to the attic to stow the quilt away yet again.

More years passed without my exploring options of transforming the quilt.

This time as Tom carried the quilt in from the attic, I knew it would be the last time. That's when I called the children in to hear the story of Grandy's quilt.

Mixing the vision of my children with the quilt and the memories of my childhood with the quilt cemented my decision. I had plans for the quilt, and this was the year to make the plans happen. With heartfelt conviction, I knew I would find a way to share this treasure with everyone who loved Grandy.

I saw how many rips remained to be patched and loose threads that needed tightening. I felt frustrated because I couldn't make the quilt whole again. I wanted to give it life once more. And most of all, I wanted my Grandy back. Oh, I didn't want Grandy the way she was when she left this world. I wanted the Grandy I remembered as a little girl. I wanted the Grandy back who saved the scraps of fabric and created this quilt. I wanted the Grandy back who talked to me through the oval mirror while she moved around her small bedroom. I thought that by giving the quilt new life, everyone in Grandy's family could enjoy a part of Grandy's quilt and her memory, ensuring she would never be forgotten.

"Mom, are you crying?" Alex asked softly.

With tears welling up in my eyes, I said, "Oh Alex, I wish I could fix the ache in my heart for my grandmother as easily as I could change this quilt."

I reached down for the end of the quilt that hung over the edge of the bed and lifted it to Alex's and Elizabeth's cheeks the way I held the same quilt to my cheeks when I was a child. I hoped they could feel the love Grandy put in her quilt as it caressed their faces.

Just then, little Gracie began stretching and making groaning sounds as she awoke. She wrinkled her nose as the quilt brushed by her face. She broke the magical spell of silence by blurting out, "Ick! What stinks so bad?"

"Well," Elizabeth explained with authority, "that's what old smells like."

My tears gave way to laughter as I mused at the wisdom of my eight-year-old. "Okay, guys, let's put our heads together and figure out what we can do with this old quilt. Wouldn't it be great if we could find a way to share it with everyone in Grandy's family?"

Three young voices piped up offering a flurry of ideas.

"We could make Christmas stockings for everyone! We'll surprise them all!" suggested Alex excitedly.

Elizabeth chimed in, "It will be the best gift."

Grace added, "We could make little mittens, too!"

"Can we make two angels for Benjamin and Daniel?" Elizabeth asked.

I was touched she remembered her twin cousins who died at birth, but had always been recognized as part of our family.

"We could make presents and give them at our family Christmas," Elizabeth offered.

"You mean *this* Christmas?" I asked.

"YES!" they all agreed.

Alex my ever-logical child said, "Since Grandy was Grandpa's mother, we could wrap the gifts all together, and Grandpa could open the present for the whole family."

This new child-imposed deadline seemed unrealistic, but they were adamant and excited about the project. I knew I would turn the world upside down, if necessary, to ensure this gift was completed on time.

I thought my biggest problem was Christmas being only two weeks away. Immediately, I realized I had a bigger problem—I couldn't sew. How would I possibly find someone who had the time, interest, and talent to transform our idea into reality? I remembered how difficult it was the last time I searched for help with the quilt.

Pursuing the transformation of the quilt anyway, I feverishly began calling friends and dug out my old list of master quilters and called each of them too. I explained to each one my urgency to complete this task. Given the tight deadline and challenge of the job, no one was available to take on this project. While I wasn't surprised at their lack of interest, I was committed to making my children's dream for Grandy's quilt come true.

I knew I couldn't give up, but discouragement still invaded my thoughts. Not knowing where to begin, I called Auntie Kaye. I felt she'd figure out a way to make this work. After all, I reasoned, Auntie Kaye could get anything done. I dialed, and she answered on the first ring. I took that as a sign that things would work out.

"Hi, Auntie Kaye, it's me, Catherine. I'm in a terrible bind over here."

She knew I tended to exaggerate and that my binds were often less traumatic than they sounded.

"How can I help?"

"Remember a few years back when I received Grandy's quilt after she died?"

"Yes, dear."

"Well, I've stored it in the attic, and in past years I've taken it to several master quilters hoping to restore it. But they've all said it would be nearly impossible to do. The kids and I have been talking, and we'd like to make it into gifts for the family. The kids suggested Christmas stockings, mittens, and angels."

"Oh, that sounds like a beautiful idea!" Auntie Kay responded.

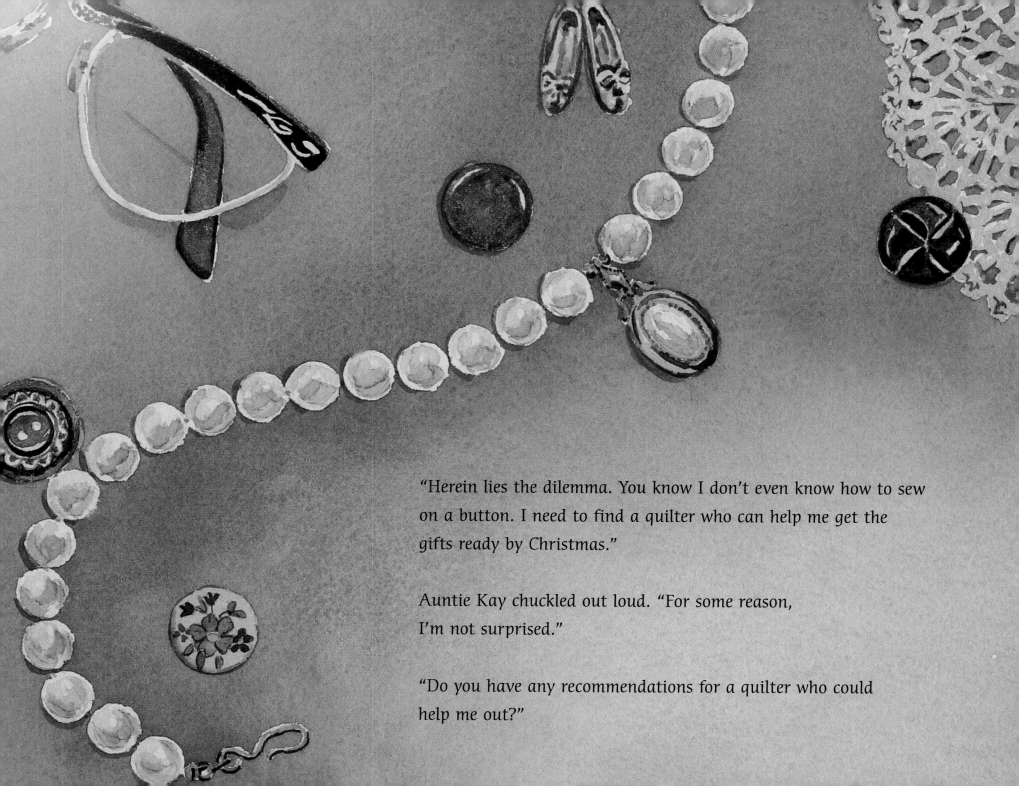

"Herein lies the dilemma. You know I don't even know how to sew on a button. I need to find a quilter who can help me get the gifts ready by Christmas."

Auntie Kay chuckled out loud. "For some reason, I'm not surprised."

"Do you have any recommendations for a quilter who could help me out?"

"Let me think for a minute."

I remained quiet as the silence on the other end of the phone grew longer.

"I do know of a woman named Mrs. Olsen. She is talented and has a love of family heirlooms. I'm not sure your timeline would fit hers, but it might be worth a try. Here is her number."

As I wrote down the phone number Auntie Kaye gave me, I was so ready to call Mrs. Olsen, I could hardly keep from shaking in anticipation. I quickly thanked Auntie Kaye, clicked off the phone, took a deep breath, and dialed Mrs. Olsen's number.

A cheerful sounding woman answered, and I rapidly rattled off, "Mrs. Olsen?"

"Yes."

"Hello, my name is Catherine. My Aunt Kaye gave me your name and told me you may be able to help me with a project. I have an heirloom quilt I was given after my grandmother passed away. It is very old and in terrible shape. I've been advised to disassemble it and make a keepsake from it. Originally, I hoped to restore it, but that doesn't seem possible anymore. I've got an idea for making keepsakes for my family and was hoping you could help me."

Nervous and not wanting her to say no, I laughed that nervous laugh and kept talking. "Well, not actually help me. I need you to make the entire transformation. I'm not skilled at sewing."

"Oh, I'm sure you're exaggerating!" Mrs. Olsen's voice was friendly and encouraging.

If she only knew how I was telling the truth, I thought.

"Do you think you could take this project on?" I gritted my teeth with worry and anticipation, and wanted to cover my ears as I dared to make the statement that would make or break the project. "And, I was hoping to have it completed by Christmas."

As I held my breath, Mrs. Olsen said, "I'd certainly be willing to take a look at what you've got."

Her next comment surprised me as she said, "Come right over, dear."

"Yes!" I said to myself. "Thank you. Thank you. Thank you!" was all I could say to her. I jotted down directions to her house, and with a dance in my step, ran to hang up the receiver.

I yelled to Tom and the children to come quick. "I've found someone willing to look at doing something with Grandy's quilt. But I have to go right away. Come, help me get Grandy's quilt back in its box."

With the quilt safely in the box and the box tucked under my arm, I grabbed my car keys and headed for the door. Stopping suddenly, I turned and ran back to the kitchen cupboard and grabbed the old coffee can filled with Grandy's items. The can stood in the same spot for years. I never thought about why I kept Grandy's can of small treasures. I just knew I'd use them for something someday.

When I looked inside I saw her old buttons, doilies, and charms, along with her glasses and assorted jewelry still there. I was so grateful everyone, including the children, left the tin alone. I took it as another sign something good was about to happen to Grandy's quilt.

I blew a goodbye kiss to my family as I ran out the door. The frigid cold confirmed the Christmas deadline was imminent. I hardly waited for the engine to warm up before heading down the winding gravel road.

I drove twenty minutes past a frozen lake, wintry woods, and open Red River Valley farmland. A small dairy farm was nestled at the end of a dirt road that ran alongside a narrow flowing creek. Snow sparkled, icicles glistened; there seemed to be magic in the air. Past the barn and the wooden sheds and over the bridge, I made my way up the snow-covered driveway.

As I opened the car door, I faced an old furry elkhound, which stood sentinel before the farmhouse with its chipped brown paint and crackled white trim. Cautiously, I looked past him, to see if anyone was about. A friendly grandmotherly face appeared from behind the opening door.

"Come in, come in," she said as she waved me inside. "His bark is much bigger than his bite. He likes to think he's the boss around here. Come on, Sparky," she called. "Let Catherine in."

The petite woman wore dark colored slacks. The pink heart quilted on her sweatshirt immediately reminded me of Grandy. I guessed Mrs. Olsen was in her early seventies. Loose gray curls surrounded her face. Her eyes twinkled, and her lips curled into a smile as I approached the open door. She moved slowly, but with a gracefulness that covered her slight limp. Her warm voice carried a hint of her Norwegian heritage. "I'm Mrs. Olsen," she said.

"I'm Catherine. Thank you so much for taking a look at my project. I know I am almost expecting a miracle to have this project finished by Christmas."

She put her hand up to stop me from apologizing. Sweeping her arm toward the open door, she ushered me the rest of the way into the house.

Stepping into her small kitchen, Mrs. Olsen motioned for me to sit at her table. The dark brown woodwork, the buckled linoleum flooring, and the kitchen clutter reminded me of Grandy's house. The aroma of a breakfast of bacon and eggs lingered in the air. It appeared this warm kitchen was the heart of her home.

"Do you like coffee, my dear?" she asked as she poured me a cup of rich coffee from a small, silver pot just taken off the stove. She still used the old-fashioned coffee pot where the grounds were mixed in the water, and the water boiled up around them to make coffee. I remember Grandy waiting just a minute before pouring coffee to give the grounds a chance to settle back to the bottom of the pot. When Mrs. Olsen poured my coffee, she did it just like Grandy did. Some of the grounds slid into the cup and swirled to the bottom, the same as they did when Grandy poured.

I took a sip and felt like I was back in Grandy's kitchen on a Sunday morning. The coffee tasted good. "This reminds me of when I was younger and my Grandy made coffee. We were allowed to drink it, but mine required sugar cubes and fresh cream brought in from the barn. By the time I drank it, it had the appearance of chocolate milk," I said.

Mrs. Olsen just smiled at me as if allowing me to absorb the feeling of contentment in her home.

As I looked around the room, my eyes noticed a small cabinet. "Mrs. Olsen, your china hutch is lovely. You have some unique pieces." There were crystal dishes, cups, saucers, and polished silver, along with ornate porcelain figurines.

"Oh, thank you, honey. They're probably not worth much, but the history of each item is priceless to me."

Mrs. Olsen's modest kitchen reminded me of Grandy's old farmhouse. I pictured bread rising and a whole fryer chicken cooking on the wood stove until the pot boiled over. I instantly felt at home. Happily and surprisingly, I found what I had been unknowingly looking for—a modern day piece of Grandy right here on earth in the form of Mrs. Olsen.

When we finished coffee, together we rolled out Grandy's tattered quilt on Mrs. Olsen's kitchen table. Her eyes lit up, then softened, as she scrutinized the quilt. I watched her move her fingers slowly across the material. Her fingers were gnarled, like Grandy's had been in her later years, attesting to years of hard work.

"Oh, Catherine, my dear," she cooed, "what a treasure you have from your Grandmother."

"I brought some other things of Grandy's," I said, as I reached for the old coffee can.

Picking out each article from the can as if it were a rare artifact, Mrs. Olsen said, "Tell me about your grandmother and her family."

"She was a strong, proud woman who was left a widow to raise two teenage boys alone on a farm. She not only farmed; she was an English teacher too." I continued proudly, "Grandy was an auditor at the court house as well. She cooked the perfect pot roast on Sundays, always followed by her lemon meringue pie that she would modestly tell us didn't turn out. And, the best part about Grandy was she always had a hug and a kiss for everyone."

Talking about Grandy to this woman who reminded me so much of her brought tears to my eyes. As I discreetly tried to wipe away my tears, I saw from the corner of my eye that Mrs. Olsen was dabbing away some tears of her own.

"Oh, honey, you must have loved your grandmother very much. This quilt represents not only your grandmother, but all your memories of her life."

Mrs. Olsen's perceptive words flew straight to my heart. It was a special moment, and it felt like we connected to each other's past, even though we'd just met.

After a thoughtful moment of silence, Mrs. Olsen spoke, "Catherine, see this square?" as she pointed to the bright purple and light blue circles.

"Uh huh," I nodded.

"Believe it or not, I made two shirts from that same fabric. And this one," she chuckled, pointing to the canary yellow and bright green flowers, "I made doll clothes from this fabric. It must have been a common, inexpensive material in its day," Mrs. Olsen commented.

"Weird, I just told my children that I had doll clothes made from that same fabric too."

As we shared our observations about the various fabrics, Mrs. Olsen began to tell me in detail about the flour sacks that were popular in the 1930s. Then she gave me her thoughts about the squares Grandy repaired and other squares that still needed to be mended.

I sensed I overwhelmed her by all the talk about Grandy and me. I felt embarrassed when I realized I didn't know a thing about her. I asked her, "Can you ever get away from the cows, milking, and chores?"

"Oh, not very often. I have an illness that prevents me from going too far, so I stick pretty close to home."

"Tell me about your children. Do they farm with you; do they live around here?"

One question led to another and before I knew it, she opened her china cabinet, and we were going through her family treasures. She shared the pieces of her own quilt of life with me. As we talked, I could tell what she deemed most important in her life. While she enjoyed her home, it wasn't the most precious thing to her. Her faith and family were.

Mrs. Olsen spoke of her husband and adult children. With a great belly laugh and a twinkle in her eye, she said, "I'm secretly trying to marry off at least one of them."

She talked of living her life, sharing that she had been ill for many years and knew she was living on borrowed time. A lump grew in my throat as she continued on, not stopping for my sympathy. Over the next hour she told more stories of her life and showed me some of the handiwork she loved to do.

My heart filled with emotion at her life story, for in it I saw acts of humility, faith, and endurance. She truly knew the blessings of life.

I thought I would hire Mrs. Olsen to help me give gifts from Grandy to my family this Christmas. Instead, during the season of giving, I received a great gift from her. Just as the Magi brought rich presents to Jesus, this wise woman gave me a priceless gift—an understanding of how to live each day filled with faith, hope, and love.

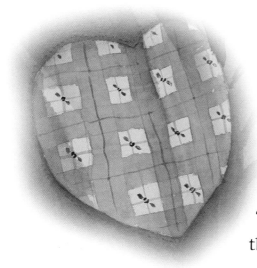

Mesmerized by how much Mrs. Olsen was like my Grandy, I felt completely at home with her. I glanced at my watch and was amazed to discover more than two hours passed since I arrived at her home. "Mrs. Olsen, I've kept you far too long, and I need to get back home." Sitting on my crossed fingers, hoping her answer to taking on my project was yes, I asked the million-dollar question. "What do you think about the project? Would you be interested in transforming the quilt for my family?"

"Catherine, I would be honored to work on your special holiday gift. What a treasure you have and how wonderful that you want to share it with others. Whoever receives this gift will know how much thought and love went into its renovation."

We made plans to utilize the children's ideas of using the quilt to make Christmas stockings, mittens, and angels. As I stood up from the table, I cast a final lingering last look at Grandy's quilt. I knew Mrs. Olsen had a big job to do in a short length of time.

Driving home, I felt on top of the world. I knew without a doubt that Mrs. Olsen would create a great memory for my family. Anything she did would be wonderful, for I had already been given my own special Christmas gift—Mrs. Olsen.

Early on Christmas Eve morning, the phone rang. "Hello, Catherine? It's Mrs. Olsen. I've finished everything in the nick of time! I'm sorry about the delay, but I wanted to make sure the gifts were as good as I could make them. What time would work for you to come and pick them up?"

I bubbled with enthusiasm, "Would now be all right?"

"Of course, Catherine, my dear. Come right over."

After a quick brush of my tangled, curly hair, I hurried to my car. I hardly dared look at the speedometer as I drove over the country roads.

Mrs. Olsen's driveway seemed longer than before. The cantankerous elkhound barked a greeting again, but this time I bounded past him to the house. When Mrs. Olsen opened the door, she ushered me into the kitchen and pointed to the chair. I sat down nervously.

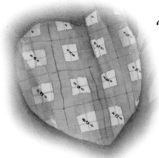

"This has been such a fun project for me," she smiled. "I hope it's okay," she said timidly.

There was her Scandinavian simplicity and humility. She brought out a bulky bag and, like a magician with a bag of tricks, she produced ten Christmas stockings, eight pairs of mittens, and two angels. I was speechless. I looked at her hard work, then at her.

"I love them all!" I exclaimed, unable to hide my excitement.

One by one I picked each gift up and pressed them to my cheek. Grandy's buttons and lace adorned the Christmas stockings. Her black octagonal wire eyeglasses were sewn by their ear pieces to one of them, her charms to another. Mrs. Olsen sewed miniature bells around each of the small angels she created. Not only had Mrs. Olsen worked her magic to bring new life to my old quilt, but she became my very own angel!

"Catherine, thank you for allowing me the opportunity to work on your family keepsake. It has been a rewarding experience. I hope your family cherishes these pieces as much as I enjoyed making them."

"Thank you, Mrs. Olsen, for giving me—all of us—the best Christmas ever."

Misty eyed again, I turned to Mrs. Olsen, "Spending time with you was like turning back the hands of time and being with Grandy again."

As I prepared to leave, she abruptly stopped me. "Oh, I almost forgot, dear. I've made you something special." She turned to go into her living room to retrieve something, and as she came around the corner, she held out a stuffed bear. "This is for you, Catherine. I made it from leftover quilt scraps. I hope you have a special place for him."

No words came, but both our tears spilled easily as we embraced. Grandy's quilt bonded the two of us together in a remarkable way.

I couldn't wait until Christmas Day when my family gathered to unwrap their special gift. I imagined their faces when they saw what had become of Grandy's quilt.

I still had work to do—final touches only I could provide. I wrote a poem about Grandy and her quilt. I wanted the Christmas stockings to be reminders of Grandy's life and the lessons she taught. Just as Grandy worked to fashion a quilt from many pieces of fabric, I weaved words together in a tribute to Grandy. I created a transfer pattern of the words to my poem, which I penned in my finest script, then carefully ironed the poem to the back of each stocking.

At last all the stockings were finished. I called my children to be a part of wrapping these special presents. Together we spread these heirloom gifts on the floor. They picked up the stockings, mittens, and angels, inspected them, and held them to their cheeks the same way I did when I first saw them at Mrs. Olsen's. I recited my poem, which they discovered when they turned the stockings over. I told them about Mrs. Olsen and how she had given a part of Grandy back to each of us.

We found a large box and lined it with beautiful gold tissue. First we placed the stockings carefully in the bottom of the box. Next came the mittens and, finally, the two angels. We added more white tissue, then put the box cover on. After wrapping the box in the brightest red and green paper we could find, we tied a bow snugly on top of it. Our gift was finally ready.

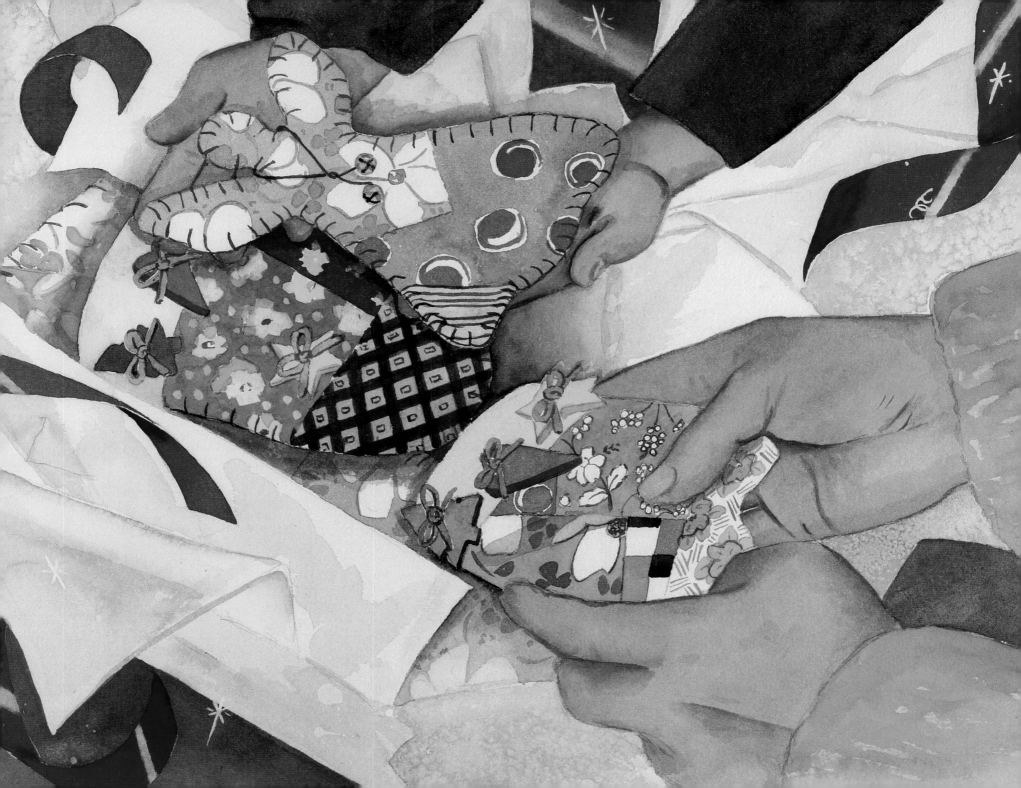

On Christmas morning, I don't know who was more excited, the children or me. We expected my entire family for the Christmas celebration. While preparing the Christmas turkey, my mind wondered off as I imagined the look on my father's face when he recognized the familiar fabrics in their new form.

All morning the children kept asking, "Is it time yet? When can we give the special gift?"

After our Christmas meal and family conversation, a piano recital by Alex, and the traditional Christmas program put on by Alex, Elizabeth, Grace, and their cousins, the time arrived.

Everyone assembled in the family room, next to the stone fireplace already stoked and ready to warm us. We opened our presents one by one and passed them around for all to see. Just when it appeared all the gifts were opened, I nodded to my children, the signal to bring out the prized package.

Alex, Elizabeth, and Grace came in procession before us with the large ornate box and laid it in the lap of their grandfather, Grandy's eldest son.

"Well,"
he exclaimed,
"what is this? Why
do I get such a large
gift all to myself?"

"Grandpa, you don't get
the whole gift to yourself.
You just get to open it for
everyone, but then you have
to share!" exclaimed Grace.

The young ones gathered at Grandpa's feet.
With wide eyes, they watched him pull apart the bow and peel away the wrapping.
As he caught sight of the treasures hidden within, he held his breath. He sat still, staring at
the treasure in amazement. It was Alex who reached into the box to bring forth a stocking, turning it so
Grandpa could read the poem about Grandy's quilt.

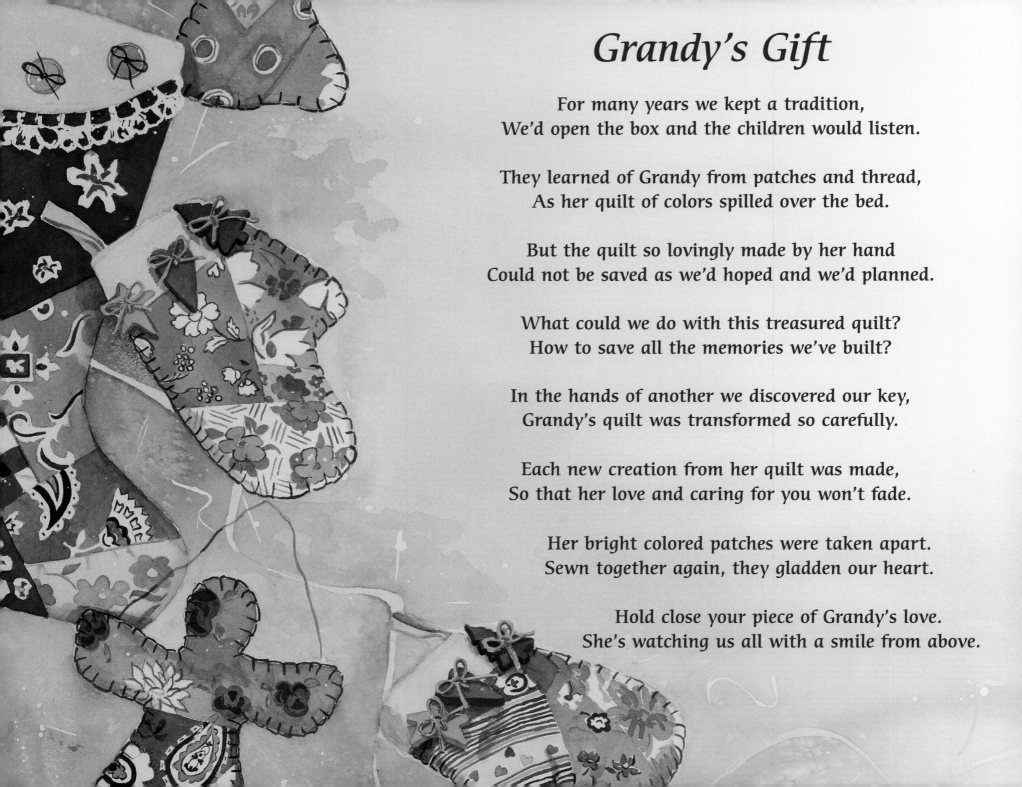

Grandy's Gift

For many years we kept a tradition,
We'd open the box and the children would listen.

They learned of Grandy from patches and thread,
As her quilt of colors spilled over the bed.

But the quilt so lovingly made by her hand
Could not be saved as we'd hoped and we'd planned.

What could we do with this treasured quilt?
How to save all the memories we've built?

In the hands of another we discovered our key,
Grandy's quilt was transformed so carefully.

Each new creation from her quilt was made,
So that her love and caring for you won't fade.

Her bright colored patches were taken apart.
Sewn together again, they gladden our heart.

Hold close your piece of Grandy's love.
She's watching us all with a smile from above.

Grace looked up at her Grandpa. Taking an angel from the box, she brought it to his cheek to gently wipe away the lone tear that trickled down his face.

Our treasured memories of Grandy's strength and faith endured in the quilt Mrs. Olsen fashioned anew for us. One used and tattered family heirloom became gifts for many. In the hush of that tender Christmas night, I looked up to the stars, thought of Grandy and Mrs. Olsen, and whispered, "Thank you."

ABOUT THE AUTHOR

Mother, wife, friend, speaker, consultant, Reneé Rongen wears many hats. Follow her now as she adds the new role of gifted writer and author. Share with Reneé this heartwarming story of her grandmother's quilt transformation and journey of discovering an extraordinary friendship in the folds.

Reneé Rongen is a nationally recognized professional speaker who has inspired thousands of people to "live life deeper." Her story has been told in numerous national magazines, newspapers, and television and radio interviews. Reneé's greatest privilege is being wife and mother. She makes her home with them on a peaceful, northern Minnesota lake.

Reneé loves life and is continually challenging herself to share her gifts with others. Her goal is to be able to say at the end of her life "I come to You just as I am. I have nothing left. I used all the gifts You gave me."

For more information about Reneé or to book her for your upcoming speaking engagements, please contact her at:
http://www.reneerongen.com • renee@reneerongen.com • 218-687-2593.

ABOUT THE ILLUSTRATOR

Mary J. Maguire graduated from the College of St. Norbert. After a grand tour of Europe, she continued her art education at the University of Minnesota and the Minneapolis College of Art and Design. Ms. Maguire has done book illustration, giftware design, and numerous commissioned paintings. She resides with her family in St. Paul, Minnesota.

ORDER INFORMATION

To order additional copies of
Grandy's Quilt — A Gift for All Seasons
please visit www.reneerongen.com